101 Reasons to Leave New York

by

Howard Jordan, Jr.

Strategic Book Publishing and Rights Co.

Strategic Book Group
12620 FM 1960, Suite A4-507
Houston, TX 77065
www.sbpra.com

ISBN: 978-1-62516-256-4

Design: Dedicated Book Services (www.netdbs.com)

Dedication

*T*his little book about the big city is dedicated to all the people who have made my life better, regardless of when and where we happened to have crossed paths. However, special love is directed squarely at my NYC family. You took me in and never let me go. This means you, Jenna, Shameka, Stacy, Marcel, Musa, Malcolm, Chad, Bin, Tamara, Sabrina, Randall and Erin.

*F*irst, let's establish a couple of ground rules. In this book and in this city, *New York* refers to Manhattan and very specific cool-ass parts of Brooklyn. *You* refers to anyone who has willingly come to the Big Apple through hard work, big dreams, or a combination of both.

You stayed up late fantasizing about the city that never sleeps. So, living the dream isn't only having a 212 area code (646, 718, 917 and 347 count, too). It's waking up every day knowing your job, life's ambition, and most closely held desires can't be experienced on this high a level, with this type of intensity, with such potential for reward and recognition, anywhere else on the planet.

Simply put, New York City is the Mecca of dreamers, seers, visionaries, freaks, geeks, cool kids, and sexy valedictorians. And so you've come. You aren't so much welcomed as invited to migrate to New York to find fame, fortune, love, acceptance, and most importantly, yourself. That, in the quickest and broadest of strokes, is the lure, the potential, the reality and beauty of New York.

It's simply amazing. But— and New York City is all about the *but*—what happens when the clock goes around, the calendar flips, and your lover, New York, reveals itself to be something else? What happens when those cute little idiosyncrasies you once loved become intolerable habits that can absolutely drive you up the wall?

This isn't about just surviving in New York City. This is about indulging, chasing, catching, and enjoying all the facets of the New York City dream, whatever yours may be. But then suddenly, you wake up one morning or early afternoon, only to realize you might not want to be here anymore.

Of course, *might* is the same energy of uncertainty that brought you here in the first place. So *might* may be what keeps you here. But if not New York City, then who? Oops—if not New York City, then where?

No place is, or could ever be, what New York City is. It changes you and changes with you. It's the backdrop of your most innocent remembrances, as well as your most satisfyingly devious endeavors. Yet, more and more often, you entertain the idea of leaving. You know you're spoiled by the New York-ness of your existence, but you don't revel in it as fully as you once did. And worse, you don't care to.

It's not just growing up; it's more like growing out. If you knew where to go, you'd already be gone. Instead, you wrestle with the idea that New York City, your mysterious, fantastical dream companion, has become nothing more than a roommate to whom you're no longer attracted and with whom you aren't even certain you're friends.

So, for all of you who have lived it, to all of those who dream of doing so one day, to everyone in the midst of it at this very moment, and to anyone who may be interested in this very specific struggle: this is a book that recognizes and articulates the unimaginable notion of willingly leaving New York City, then gives all the reasons you'll ever need to justify doing so— in no particular order, but somewhat categorized for your convenience.

You're welcome.

1. The best part about living here is telling people who don't that you do.

Bling-bling! Bling-bling! When you wear New York City, you shine, you sparkle, you glow, and utterly, you steal the show. It's social jewelry, cultural clout, and it's unmistakable.

It's conversational cache. When you talk about the greatness of New York, the inspiration of New York, and you wax poetic to those who can only wish they lived here, you know their imaginations and attentions are fully captured. And you love it!

After all, membership does have its privileges. But it comes at a price.

Lately, you've noticed the New York City you're selling to the huddled masses is no longer the New York City you've been buying into. For as amazingly satisfying and ridiculously stimulating you tell them New York City is, you've begun to realize it's rarely either of those things to you anymore.

2. You can't enjoy movies set in New York.

Movies are all about escaping daily life and falling away from everything familiar to you. For full enjoyment, you need to forget where you are and embrace the total suspension of disbelief.

But when streets don't connect, timing is improbable, and the so-called New York City on screen isn't very New York at all, you can't enjoy the experience the way you want to. You may not know the city like the back of your hand. But clearly, you know it better than the second-unit director and his two assistants who worked on the last two action movies you've seen.

3. Someone else does your laundry and you're not rich.

Maybe your building doesn't have washers and dryers, or maybe they don't have enough. It's understandable that you think the laundry room is too dark, crowded, or creepy looking. Plus, you don't want to waste a few hours separating whites, colors, and delicates. However, you know you should be cleaning your own sheets.

The fact that you don't and you don't see a problem with it says something about you. But as long as there is starch in your collars and not too much bleach in your whites, you couldn't care less.

4. You've kind of forgotten how to drive.

At first, it's an unexpected luxury. Mass transit: trains, buses, cabs, and don't forget walking, biking, rollerblading, skateboarding, and the fact that everywhere you're supposed to be is relatively close to where you already are.

Then, on a visit home, an out-of-town business trip, or just a night when you got roped into being the designated driver, you adjust the seat and the mirrors. You make sure everyone is buckled in. Then you realize something is very wrong.

It's eerily unfamiliar and a bit scarier than you remember. So you position your hands firmly at ten and two and turn the radio down, if not off, so you can concentrate more than you ever did in Driver's Ed.

5. You're afraid of the J and Z trains.

With all the colors in the spectrum and with all the options available to the art directors employed by the MTA, why in the hell would they choose brown as the key color for the express trains to the Twilight Zone?

Maybe those tracks don't lead to an alternate dimension, but they might as well, because you rarely see the J and Z trains.

You refuse to ride them and you have no idea where they actually go. They're mysterious, and thus, their untold power is to be respected. Are they the passageway to the land of poltergeists, or the trains to Beetlejuice's house? You don't know and you're not trying to find out.

6. People don't cover their mouths when they sneeze.

Supposedly worldly, socially experienced, and politically savvy New Yorkers are also a bunch of sicky-poo, cootie-bug, virus spreaders. There's the coughing, nose-blowing, and, of course, the wettest of transgressions: sneezing.

How could they? How dare they? So many shared spaces and objects with so little opportunity to escape. It's just not right. Yet it happens all too regularly.

Nasty stares and spiteful glares do nothing. Only an old-fashioned "Cover your damned mouth!" will suffice. But at what risk?

This is New York City. It could be an invitation to disaster. Whatever it is, it's disgusting. It's also the reason you can't get over your damned cold, assuming it's just a cold.

7. Subway breezes.

On those hot and humid dog days of New York City summers, you've actually taken short-lived refuge in those precious seconds on the subway platform as the approaching train kicks up a wind that pushes down the track and directly into your face.

You bask in the glory.

In your mind, you're posing like the statue of Jesus Christ that overlooks Rio de Janeiro. You bathe in the airborne filth and debris, fanning out the wet spots in your shirt, all while holding your breath, gritting your teeth, and keeping your mouth firmly sealed.

It's so dirty, but it's so good. Just the way you like it.

8. You need more space, mental or otherwise.

There's hardly enough space to walk down the street without someone touching you or to be on the subway without someone rubbing up against you. You can barely walk through your own apartment without bumping into the bed or having to step over something else.

Physically, you've learned to deal. But the lack of space to simply *be* has gradually made it more difficult to find the wherewithal to cope.

9. You can't live in Central Park.

There is nothing wrong with it. Anything goes and everyone does!

There's sun. There's shade. It's clean. It's brimming with love and peace. Joy and laughter. Acceptance beyond tolerance. Flavor and style. Tourists and natives living in glorious harmony. Benches and even a little space to stretch out.

Friends, relatives, and perfect strangers walking hand in hand, enjoying the bohemian excellence of the structural beauty of the Bethesda Fountain, Delacorte Theater, and the wonder of city planning at its artistic and pragmatic zenith. All at the pace that best suits you.

But it's seasonal. It closes. It's a reminder of what New York could and should be, if the people in it could take its general state of being with them as they disperse throughout the rest of the city.

10. *HGTV*.

It's unbelievable what they can do with a home. It's slightly more unbelievable what they can do to your psyche. The homes and the gardens are better than anything you'll call your own as long as you have a New York City zip code, assuming you don't hit the Mega Millions jackpot.

You're envious of the way they can turn any old space into a brand-new living experience. You're jealous of how little land and contractors cost in comparison to everything you know to be true about New York City real estate.

You also know that if you're going to give up New York, or give up on it, you'll need a big, beautiful, ridiculously comfortable and well-designed home and garden, because wherever you go to get it, you'll be spending a lot of time in it. There won't be anything else to do but shop for marble flooring, chandeliers, and countertops.

11. It feels as if the buildings are leaning in on you.

New York City is a rat race, a shark tank, and a meat market. It's also a romance novel just waiting to be written, starring you and the sexy-guilty-pleasure love interest of your choosing. That's why you love it.

It's also why you're tormented by it at the very same time. Lately, when you look up, you feel a little down. The buildings have seemingly morphed from glorious high rises to electric containment fences, and the night sky is more of a ceiling than a gateway to another world. You don't question the structural integrity of the buildings above and around you. You know they're not going anywhere.

But can the same still be said about you? Because what's the point in living amongst skyscrapers if you're no longer certain you belong amongst the stars?

12. You want to test the "You can make it anywhere" part of the song.

Most people think you don't really leave New York City; you get knocked out, driven out, or thrown out, beaten so completely you welcome the move.

However, it is possible to simply want a new frontier to explore and conquer. New York City is the ultimate proving ground. Elsewhere, where some things are givens, where lazy Tuesdays exist and you can actually hear the birds singing without trying to do so, it must be easier.

After all you've been through to survive and thrive this unforgiving, perilous urban jungle, everywhere else has to seem like a kid-friendly, heavily padded jungle gym.

13. The crappy little parks have actually begun to feel like nice little parks.

Come on, you know better. A patch of grass with a few chairs in the middle of an intersection does not a park make. Well kept. Crowded as hell.

No matter where you once called home, you've enjoyed parks where you can't see or hear traffic from any point within them.

A real park has trails on which you'd be hard pressed to see someone else and multiple playgrounds where children and adults can frolic. Now every chance you get, you try to take a mini-vacation by seeking out a spot to sit and bathe in the exhaust of passing cars in a tiny little park that really isn't one at all.

14. You'd like to stand still without feeling as though you're being passed by.

By nature, if not by design, New York City is transient. People, ideas, dreams, and expectations come and go in a constant parade of sensory inundation, and you absolutely love it. Right up until you don't. Then what?

Do you make the decision to love the experience for what it's worth, or move on in search of more permanent place to call home?

To indulge and appreciate New York City is to understand and embrace a life for rent. It is to become completely comfortable with always being at least a little uncomfortable. It is to accept that living here requires you to be in perpetual motion and demands constant reinvention. And even then, success is not guaranteed. It is to come to terms with the idea that you deserve nothing more than you get. Furthermore nothing you get will ever truly be yours and yours alone.

15. Tomorrow ain't looking any better.

Screw Little Orphan Annie. She had no idea what she was talking about. She was eight years old; what did she know?

The sun isn't coming out tomorrow.

You've been bright-eyed and bushy-tailed on quite a few occasions, only to end up black-eyed with your tail between your legs.

But New York City isn't rain or shine. It's both, all the time.

The best you can hope for is a strong umbrella when a shower hits. You can stay safe and dry inside with far less guilt and for far less money in so many other cities. Maybe it's time you did.

Just remember, you can't have rainbows without the rain, and without the rainbow, there's no pot of gold.

16. You're no longer satisfied with never being satisfied.

You came here to have something, to be something, to experience something unique to New York City. It's that curiosity that fuels the success-yielding fire to do what it takes to get what you want.

So no matter what you do or get done, it will never be enough.

You get a promotion. It should have come sooner and with more money. You get a new place. It's in the wrong neighborhood. You catch the only available cab on a rainy Thursday during the evening rush. It doesn't smell fresh enough. You receive a compliment. It wasn't complimentary enough.

However, when you stop scrambling long enough to consider all of the things you've chased and captured, you realize satisfaction may never be among them.

On the other hand, that does give you something else to strive for. Doesn't it?

17. You've had all you can stand and you can't stand no more.

The fight. Either you're taking it to someone (or something), or they're taking it to you. You've gotten used to it. Your record shows more wins than losses. But of late, you seem to be taking more punishment than you're dishing out.

Your reflexes have deteriorated considerably, and you may be a touch punch-drunk. You don't have the hunger you once possessed, and there are a lot of young guns waiting to take a shot.

Either move to the side, or get knocked out of the way if you choose to stay. But do you know how to watch from the sidelines when you're used to being one of the biggest players in the game? Or would you be more inclined to make one last run?

18. The cost of doing business.

When is nothing just nothing? Never. Not here. It hasn't been and it never will be. Every move means something and every static moment does as well.

First, you have to accept and respect that. Then, figure out how much spiritual currency you have at your disposal and just how much you are willing to spend.

New York City is a place of luxury and excess. So don't behave like those contestants on the early days of *Wheel of Fortune,* buying ceramic dogs and cuckoo clocks.

If you're going to sell out, lease out, or any other version of it, get your money's worth. New York City is no place for those on a budget of any kind. Those fond of belt tightening need not apply.

19. You wake up sad.

Even Olympic hurdlers run at least 10 meters between jumps. But in New York City, you can't make it three steps

outside your door without having to overcome an obstacle
or two.

There was a time when your alarm clock went off—
assuming you didn't wake up naturally before it—and you
couldn't wait to get up and get at it. But of late, you spend
more time asking *why,* rather than *how.*

The worst part about being sad is that it makes you mad.
You know what lies ahead and you don't like it. It's hard
to go out and fight when you already feel defeated. Maybe
you should entertain the possibility of facing a newer, less
combative opponent.

But where's the fun in that?

20. *Your area of expertise hasn't made you rich.*

What you know plus $2.25, as of 2010, will get you
a ride on the subway. Of course, there's more to life than
money. That's the point.

What kind of life is frustration, unrecognized greatness,
and rationed meals? (No, really, if you know the answer
and can articulate it, share! Then your expertise *could* make
you rich, because this city is brimming with people who are
trying to decide how much suffering is required and how
much they're willing to endure. They'd surely pay a king's
ransom to someone who can provide some useful direction
and proven results to what has shown itself to be a land of
missed opportunities.)

Basically, life in New York City comes down to this:
build a better mousetrap or stay on the hamster wheel.

21. *Just making it isn't good enough, anymore.*

For most, the New York City experience is day to day, week to week, month to month, and hand to mouth. So you quickly learn to evaluate it as such. As long as you're living it up and turning it out, it's all fine and dandy.

But—and New York City is all about the *but*—what happens when you decide you want more?

Obviously, that all depends on your definition of *more,* since New York City is the capital of the world, boasting a higher concentration of culture, art, industry, and opportunity, not to mention love, sex, and food. (Pick up a brochure for a complete listing.)

There are countless ways to have more. But if your *more* is a slower pace, peace and quiet, or a well-priced acre or two to raise organic cattle, you're in the wrong place.

22. *You can't find your scene.*

If you can't find your scene or you've grown out of the one you once had, get out, seek, and ye shall find.

Shake hands, kiss babies, and knock on doors.

If it sounds like work, it is. If it sounds like a hustle, it is. But all you have to do is keep your ear to the ground, because your scene and your people are out there, and they're waiting for you to join the party.

If you're tired of searching for it and for them, they probably wouldn't let you in anyway. Because what kind of scene welcomes a new member who doesn't really want to be seen?

23. *You just can't catch a break.*

Basically, you've gone as far as you can go. The path is blocked and there's no way around it. You're stuck.

It's not for lack of trying. You've done all you can do. You've clawed, you've fought, and you've scratched. You've reached your ceiling and your breaking point.

So maybe it's time to sublet the apartment and teach English in Ecuador or something like that. Or take the title, the talent, and the vision you've cultivated in New York somewhere you will be properly respected, compensated, and appreciated.

New York City isn't going anywhere. But more importantly, where are *you* going if you stay?

24. *Goldilocks thinks you're hard to please.*

Nowadays, if something isn't perfect and exactly how you imagined, you're not interested. It doesn't much matter what *it* is, as long as *it* is superb in every way.

It's all about you and getting yours.

Every offer is merely the starting point of a negotiation, professionally, socially, and in every other way possible. You're ready to pass on any offer if your checklist isn't fully satisfied. But can it be? At this point, if there were such a thing as *just right*, you probably wouldn't recognize it.

25. *Your MP3 player is too bulky.*

Whether it's all about the look, or if it's knowing you have to carry everything you may possibly need for the day from dawn 'til dusk, you just want to carry less weight. When the nano isn't nano enough; when your cell phone with Internet, data, text and calendar is laughably tiny, but still cumbersome; you sometimes catch a reflection of yourself in the LCD screen and ask, WTF?

It's beyond the point of LOL but not serious enough to declare FTW. It seems a little crazy but, like everyone else in this city, you're just looking for an opportunity to upgrade.

26. *You're easily upset by subpar crème brûlée or French onion soup.*

You're familiar with the term *acquired taste* because you've acquired quite a few. You've tasted, sampled, and indulged in the best, richest, most savory dishes that executive chefs, fry cooks, and pastry gods throughout this city have to offer.

You were once just happy to eat. Now, you've developed quite the discriminating palate. You know what's good and what subtle improvements are required to attain greatness. And while you may not comment aloud

every time, pushing a dish to the side, crinkling your
nose, or uttering the always useful "That's not as good as
I expected" are unmistakable indicators that neither your
mind nor your taste buds are being blown.

Because, simply put, you've had better.

27. Everything takes too long.

To you, the phrase *short and sweet* could be a touch
shorter and slightly sweeter.

Getting to the point is the only point that matters, and
the starting line and the finish line are way too far apart.
Even though we're always moving at the speed of light and
searching for the quickest fix, instant gratification is a luxury
most aren't afforded.

In a New York minute, you should have learned that
the only thing you get by rushing is frustrated. But you
probably missed that lesson because you were in too big a
hurry.

God is in the details, and paying attention to detail
is meticulous work. But you keep switching jobs—
figuratively speaking, of course.

28. You promised yourself you'd never stay in an abusive relationship.

When New York City hits you, you make excuses for
it. When your friends tell you to leave, you tell them they

don't understand. You tell them New York loves you. You insist it was your fault. Surely you said or did something to set it off.

So, with your arm in a sling and your swollen eyes hidden behind fashionable sunglasses, you try to be everything New York City wants and nothing that it doesn't.

You keep your mouth shut and your head down, because you love it and you want to believe it won't hurt you again. But inside, you know it probably will. You can pack a bag, find shelter, and change your number, or you could choose to fight back—assuming there's any fight left in you.

29. *Freelancing is overrated.*

When it's first made an available and viable option, the idea of working for an outrageous day rate, for whomever you want, while making your own schedule, is an amazing thing. But when you're booking gigs, you have no time for anything else. When you're not booking, you wish you were.

It can be great. It can also be a great disappointment.

Over time, we all need some certainty. Believe it or not, we even need a few coworkers to talk to and have lunch with, not to mention full-coverage, group health insurance that doesn't deny or limit claims on pre-existing conditions. Just one of the benefits of having benefits.

30. Dating is such a chore.

Much like dating itself, there's no real poetry here. Just near misses and not-even-closes. The not-so-funny-funniest part of it all is that you keep giving it all you have while not giving it all you are.

The style, fashion, and ways of being needed to attract a date are different than those required to maintain a mate. But it's sexy, mysterious, fun, and adventurous. So you try to enjoy the ride. However, at some point, the destination becomes more of a pressing concern than the pleasant distractions along the side of the road, and you wonder if love can work in New York.

Or more accurately, if you've even been looking for it.

31. Sincerity has become an afterthought at best.

Simple, authentic communication is hard to come by in New York City. After a while, you come to accept it, and you make the conscious decision to say and do what you must. But it has left the realm of necessary evil and entered the zone of *just the way you are.*

You think, speak, and act differently, and when you take note of yourself, you don't necessarily care for some of the changes. Maybe it's because you have to constantly choose between being the con artist or the mark. Maybe it's not.

You recognize sincerity is a beautiful thing and a lovely sentiment, but have yet to figure out just how it can be used to help you dominate the world.

32. *You'd like your significant other to remain significant.*

Or maybe you'd like to find someone and stay with them long enough that they might become significant. New York City has options and opportunities in abundance. With that comes the flighty, what-else-is-out-there attitude that can make you stray, play, and run away from someone who could be worthwhile. Not to say that the current one or the next one is *the one*. But it's impossible to know when you behave like a three-year-old chasing butterflies in the park.

33. *You support everyone else's decision to leave.*

You completely understand when friends use you as their sounding board, selling their reasons for wanting to leave New York to themselves as much as they are selling them to you. You nod and even offer them more reasons to go, and you downplay any and every reason they come up with to stay put.

They may not leave on your advice. But you offer them no additional obligations to stick it out.

As you listen, you add some of their issues and concerns to your own growing list. You'll certainly be sad to see them go, but it does mean an affordable apartment will be opening up at the end of the month and now you have the inside track on it.

34. Insurance doesn't cover therapy.

Friends are great, but you don't want to burden them.
They have their own issues to sift through. So you've
classified them all as *break in case of emergency.*
Family is there for you. Father knows best and nothing
beats Mama's advice, but they're hundreds of miles away.
Besides, you're an adult now. Or at least, you'd like to be
seen as one. Your siblings just don't get it because they'd
gladly trade positions with you.

You need someone with credentials. A professional.
A shrink. But it's expensive. You can't afford to let your
mental health slide, but without the right insurance, you
can't afford to keep it up, either. If the co-pay is a bigger
source of stress than what you're coming to speak about,
you're in even more trouble than you thought.

In this city, catharsis is priceless. But catharsis
facilitated by someone qualified to lead you through it—
and legally bound to secrecy—is even more valuable.

35. Some of the insanity is just insane.

Not everything you see, do, or hear about can be wiped
clean by the phrase *it's just the way New York is.* Yet the
statement is true.

Comparing New York City to any other city is as
useless as … comparing New York City to any other city.

The second you decide to try to make sense of it, to
categorize it, to qualify it, and to reason with it, you're lost.

Not everything that happens here is magical, intellectual, entertaining, or even necessary, but the whole is greater than the sum of its parts.

So love it or learn to love it, because *it's just the way New York is.*

36. *The subway stops because of rain.*

Utterly absurd and yet unsurprising describes so much about New York City. So why wouldn't it describe the most popular method of getting around? A seven-day pass has inflated from $17 to $27 in just eight years, and the constant system failures make everyone ask, "Exactly what do the fare hikes pay for?"

It's expected, accepted, and the source of much amusement and frustration over how often it breaks down, causing interruptions and rerouting, not to mention the constant rush-hour maintenance. But what the hell are they doing down there?

They call it *mass transportation. Mass confusion* might be more accurate.

37. *You're thinking about going back to a job you quit.*

You loathed the gig. You couldn't stand a great number of your coworkers. So you left. You found work elsewhere. You made a conscious effort to discover yourself and what makes you happy.

You traveled, took guitar lessons, or kept a journal, and you never thought anything bad about the decision. Now some time has passed. You're thinking it wouldn't be so bad to go back. In fact, you can't even remember why you quit in the first place.

With the steady money, you suspect you'd be so much better off financially and thus emotionally. You can adapt to the office politics. You can better compartmentalize the job because you have so much more going on in your life now, right? No really, you can.

It'll all be different now! Yeah, right.

38. Other people's conversations.

In general, people are shallow, annoying, boring, misguided, and messed up in the head.

In other places, that would be more of an assumption than a proven fact. But in New York City, people are always within earshot. Their conversations are thrust upon you every time you venture out of your home: the folks sitting next to you on the train, the couple on the blanket next to yours in the park, the wait staff at your favorite burger joint, your cabbie stopping to curse out a pedestrian, and don't forget the guy on his cell in the movie theater.

It's a mishmash of inane, unimportant conversations. Yet the subjects are so critical to the lives of the participants that they must be talked about right now. Not that all conversations need be geopolitical, socioeconomic discourse, but they should at least be worth having, especially if you have to hear it.

39. Play is work.

You have to make time to play. You have to commit to it and be diligent about it. You need to clock in and refuse to quit early. You need to schedule something to get the most out of it.

Trying to relax can really stress you out, because you don't know when you'll have time to do it again. Plus, to make time, you have to take time from something else. And damn it all if your time isn't as fun as you hoped it would have been. Well, that's just a waste.

40. Gentrification seems natural.

The perfect move is to a neighborhood that is on the rise but hasn't truly risen.

Let's take the Cobble Hill and Carroll Gardens area, circa 1999. There were only two bars and one restaurant. Now it's destination eating and shopping along Smith Street and destination living for those too hip for Park Slope, quicker than those in Fort Greene, and too damn smart for the East Village.

The rent went way, way up; the ethnic groups moved out; and the once dangerous stretch along the F, between Bergen and Smith/9th, is beautiful, safe, and desired.

But, as long as people are impressed when they hear
your address, you don't care one bit about what the
neighborhood used to look like, or who used to live there.

41. Panhandlers have to earn it.

When you first moved to New York, you were moved
by the less fortunate. Now you won't even move out of
their way.

Beyond the idea that you shouldn't pull out a wad of cash
in front of a panhandler, your bigger issue when considering
giving to their cause is that you think to yourself, "Sorry, but
I work for my money. You should work for yours."

Holding out a cup isn't good enough, and a hard-luck
sob story means nothing to you, because you can't help
but think they're probably lying anyway. Still, you're not
completely made of stone. Some well-performed singing or
dancing in a moment when you have a soft heart and some
loose change may lead to a contribution.

Then again, it may not.

42. Ambivalence, apathy, or whatever.

You could keep doing it, but you're fairly certain you
don't want to. It takes either too much or too little of you.
It's too much strain and effort or too little of who you'd
truly like to be.

The thrill is gone. You don't know where it went or
when it left. You're not trying to get it back, either. It's

whatever. It's blah of the highest order. But you know if you stand in the middle of the road for too long in New York City, you will get hit by a taxi. You have to pick a side. If not, you're just passing through, taking in the sights.

Basically, you're a tourist. And you definitely don't want to be one of them.

43. Encores.

You have nothing more to give, yet the show goes on. At this point, you need the spotlight and live for the applause. If you lived anywhere else, you'd have already gone on to bigger and better things. But since you're already on the grandest stage, headlining along the Great White Way, everything else seems like dinner theater.

It represents a fall from grace, regardless of how softly you might land.

You could always take the show on the road; relearn how to appreciate the small things, the not-so-shiny things; and reconnect with the innocent idealist you used to be and wish you still were.

There's only one problem. You have a show to do.

44. You've been spending far too much time in your apartment.

If you'd rather be inside than out and about on a day Homeland Security hasn't deemed potentially disastrous, you're in the wrong city. If you go to bed early and get up late, you're in the wrong city. If you're spending enough time in your apartment to notice how small it is, you're in the wrong city. If once you get home in the evening, you're in for the night, you're in the wrong city.

If you needed any of the preceding examples to determine if you're in the right city, you're in the wrong city.

New York is too vibrant and too dynamic to hide from it. The entire city is a refuge from the rest of the world. So if you're looking to avoid it, anywhere else will do nicely.

45. You're moderate.

In political circles, New York City has often been characterized as home to holier-than-thou, out-of-touch, social elitists trying to force-feed the rest of the country an ineffective and ungodly ideal.

As a transplant from some other state, there's a chance you sometimes agree. But you can't say so. You can't be anything but to the left, even though you do have some moderate views here and there.

So if you'd like to openly express your occasionally less-than-progressive opinions without ire, a red state may be out of the question, but a lighter shade of blue may be the perfect solution.

Or you could take full advantage of those tiny little voting booth curtains. That is what they're there for, anyhow. That way, your true colors can be on full display when and where it matters most and nobody has to know.

46. The mind is willing, but the body isn't able.

When you try to conjure up the roar you once summoned at will, the best you can muster is a domesticated "meow."

Whether it's a failed attempt at a late dinner and clubbing until the sun comes up, or your inability to feign laughter or interest in a conversation with your boss, your energy is down and it happened on your watch.

Hopefully it's an acceptable, even welcomed, result of lessons learned. Maybe it's a more ominous, undesired taming.

One thing is for sure: it's you now.

47. You're a good person, but you'd like to be better.

There's a difference between good-hearted and foolhardy.

To make it amongst alpha beasts, you have to operate within the rules of the wild. So you neatly wrap your morals and set them aside when they don't serve you in any given situation. You don't want to do it, and you know every time you do, it becomes easier to do it again.

On occasion, you wonder if conditional morality is a convenient loophole, verbal gymnastics, or survival of the fittest. But living in New York City without it makes it that much more difficult for good people to do good for themselves or anybody else.

48. You can't stop cursing.

You get upset, agitated, bugged out, and pissed off much more easily than you once did. It's mostly triggered by things you've seen enough to predict the outcome. You can even predict when they'll next occur, but still, you let the expletives fly.

Later, you laugh about just how silly and immature you've been. You even swear not to do it again . . . until the next time the person in front of you at the pharmacy decides to open a new account and fill every prescription known to man, when all you want and all you need is your Xanax, Zoloft, Ambien, or birth control refill—which you can see sitting right behind the counter, wrapped, stickered, and ready to go.

But it's first come, first serve, and this S.O.B. is taking all day. Motherf*****!

49. You have no desire to "Save the Children" and you want to fight "Greenpeace".

It's nothing personal. Obviously, they're great organizations. They're doing God's work. But you don't have time to fill out surveys or answer a few questions for charity. It's not that you don't care. It's just that you don't care enough right now.

So when those reverent, earnest, hopeful college kids with dreams of saving the world approach you on the sidewalk, you sidestep them like a professional quarterback avoiding an unblocked linebacker, or you cross the street half a block earlier than you need to in order to avoid them completely.

There was a time when you'd have stopped. But that was a long time ago.

50. *You and your god don't speak often enough.*

You've become too smart and too self-reliant for your own good.

Science has trumped faith. And what you can touch has supplanted all you can feel. New York is a good time, but it can be hard living. So, for practical and understandable reasons, you've surrendered to the belief that you are the only person you can trust. But in doing so, you've forgotten all about your higher power.

Perhaps you haven't quite forgotten, but you shelved it so you could pack more lightly and be more morally aerodynamic in your journey. After all, your code and your faith are under attack from outside forces at an unbelievable rate. So you keep them locked safely away. But lately, you're opening that vault much less often, and you're having a harder time remembering the combination.

Everything is safe and secure on the inside, but how are you doing out here?

51. *You've become a little more racist.*

In a city where a minute lasts less than sixty seconds, you try to save time whenever you can. So stereotypes and generalizations are quite useful.

It doesn't take a ticket to *Avenue Q* or a DVD rental of *Crash* to realize we're all, at the very least, a little bit racist. What it might take is a split second of thought at the sight of a black guy on the basketball court, a white man with a badge, an Asian behind the wheel of a car, a Jew at a diamond store, a Middle Eastern cabbie, or a Korean store owner.

You may have come to New York for a better life, more liberty, and a higher degree of happiness. But, you did bring a few assumptions and prejudices along with you from back home. Then, promptly stirred them into this great melting pot. This city can help you undo and unlearn all of that. But it doesn't always.

In fact, from time to time, you may be reaching deeper into the darker parts of your enlightened self, even if you're the only one who knows it.

52. *Tick-tock. Tick-tock.*

The longer you stay, the harder it becomes to leave.

This town is like cultural quicksand. The more you struggle, the more entrenched you become. More than the comfort and routine of what you've come to call your home, you can't help but believe New York City is going to take a turn for the better, regardless of how good or bad things currently are.

Every time the sun rises, shining on the tired faces of after-party aficionados and walk-of-shamers, you smile. Maybe for just a moment; maybe it lasts all day. But because of the unpredictability of this routine, you're willing to hope.

Even if potential is never actualized, you can't help but think that it's just a matter of time.

53. Everything used to be something else.

You've aged, either gracefully or kicking and screaming every step of the way.

Now, the clubs you used to go to are pet stores. Interns, one of which you used to be, now look at you with an odd mix of disbelief and wonder because you finished college before they finished middle school, and you spend most of the day uncomfortably trying to laugh it off.

And the neighborhoods! Oh, the neighborhoods. Even the most dangerous ones now have enough *Time Out* and *Zagat* write-ups to blow the lid off of anything that once qualified as a best-kept secret.

Just think, there was a time you thought Maclaren was an English automobile manufacturer and Bugaboo was some type of racial slur. But thanks to the young couple chatting at the table next to you in the newly opened Starbucks that used to be a shoe store, you know better.

54. Your trainer, your favorite DJ, and your therapist have all abandoned you.

There was a time when the idea of a therapist was no more than a silly notion; a trainer was a waste of money; and DJs were a dime a dozen, because how hard can it be to spin the perfect mix of house, drum and bass, and early '90s hip-hop?

Now, you've come to respect and need all three.

But, they've either retired, left town or just stopped doing what you've become dependent upon them doing. Or maybe they decided to chase their dreams and live their lives, with little-to-no regard for yours.

Selfish bastards.

55. You've lost your hookup.

Your booty call is in a legitimate relationship. Your familiar-faced bouncer at your favorite hot-spot got fired. Your loose-with-the-liquor favorite neighborhood bartender quit because he got a role in an off-off-Broadway production. Your friend with the car got divorced and lost it in the settlement.

Your other booty call wants a serious commitment. Your friend with all the good tickets is saving to buy a condo. Basically, you've been slowly deprived of all the things that make your New York City experience such an experience. Not to mention how your last-ditch, other-other booty call recently found religion and no longer believes in casual sex.

56. *You get waaay too excited by trips to Fairway.*

Okay. You like fresh groceries. Fine. You like to cook. But how did fruit and vegetable shopping become such a highly anticipated, quasi-erotic, euphoria-inducing experience?

You've mapped the bus routes and paid proper attention to weekend maintenance changes as well as free transfers. You've verified the weekend subway schedule, and all your friends are getting up early to meet you at the station.

You may even get a Zipcar because you're considering dashing off to IKEA afterwards if your hearts don't explode from the anticipation and excitement. But even if you subscribe to the belief that life in New York City is all about finding joy in the small things, shouldn't there be a mandatory minimum on the bigness of the smallness?

Or maybe that's just New York talking.

57. *Sometimes you feel as though you're living on an island.*

Obviously, New York is a series of islands connected by trains and bridges, by accents and social classifications, but relative to the actual acreage, it's a lot of damn people in one small space. Yet for all the lights, crowds, bells, and whistles, it's remarkably easy and all too familiar a sensation to simply feel alone.

Physically, that couldn't be further from the truth. But emotionally, it can be the case.

Everyone is so caught up in his or her own New York.
They don't have a moment to get, or an interest in getting,
caught up in yours. Yes, you understand. But that doesn't
make it any easier.

It just depends on how often you experience it, how long
it lasts, and if you can handle feeling like a single castaway
stranded on an island with over eight million other survivors.

58. You never see your friends anyway.

For some reason you can go three or more months
without actually seeing the people you love. Not the fake,
European kiss-kiss, "I'm so surprised to see you here. We
should make plans to get coffee and catch up" kind of love.
But the people you honestly can't do without.

The people you absolutely respect and adore. The
people you feel blessed to know.

However, they're not keeping you here. You can text,
Tweet, and Facebook them from anywhere. In fact, they
may have already moved; you wouldn't even know it.

59. You'd like to see your family more.

If you're not careful, the pace and the *way* of New
York City can swallow you up. If it doesn't devour your
professional and/or social lives, then it will certainly get to
your family life.

There simply aren't enough hours in the day, or days in
the week, because it's always something.

You know you should make time to go home to visit the family. You want to see how your little nieces and nephews have gotten even bigger than they look in the photographs you're invited to view on Snapfish and Flickr.

It would do your soul good and give you a little perspective on just how fleeting and precious life is to sit and talk with Grandma, Grandpa, and all the cousins you only see once in a blue moon.

You know it would. But hell, you might miss something here.

60. Eye contact.

In most parts of the civilized world, when crossing paths with another human being, it's only natural to acknowledge them and have them reciprocate the gesture. But not here. In fact, the opposite applies.

Eye contact in New York is a little bit offensive. It could even be taken as an act of aggression. "Why are you looking at me?" takes the place of "Why is that person ignoring me?"

At first, it may not seem like a big deal. You consider it another one of the many little adjustments you make to live in the big city. But it has a major ripple effect through other aspects of your New York City life.

What it can do is make you feel isolated, if not altogether irrelevant from time to time. You want to be seen and noticed. But sometimes, in New York City, you won't be, because this is a world all its own.

61. *Re-introductions are so awkward.*

It happens. In fact, it keeps happening. You've met someone in passing at a dinner party, in a business meeting, in line at the Apple Store, or at the table next to you at your favorite restaurant. Then, upon unexpectedly seeing them again, you can't remember their name or anything you so deeply discussed.

Why would you?

You meet lots of people. So you stutter, stammer, and struggle to reconnect the dots of a distant and insignificant back-story in order to figure out where you encountered them, while simultaneously praying you never will again. Because as strange as it sounds, you know you won't remember them the next time you cross paths, either.

62. *Nothing surprises you, good or bad—and that's bad.*

If you live in New York City long enough, it's inevitable that you will catch a severe case of the *is-that-all-you-gots*. It may take a few months. It may take a several years. But it will happen.

It strikes without warning and your innocence and awe are instant casualties. You know you have it when it doesn't just take *more* to get and hold your attention. It takes everything at once to even warrant a second glance.

A 13-year-old female Irish cartoonist in Union Square is nice, but if she's not on fire, sparring bare-knuckled with Mike Tyson, and reading Kurt Vonnegut's *Cat's Cradle* aloud at the same time, then what's the big deal?

Most people readily admit they haven't seen it all. But once you've lived here long enough, you're not most people.

63. Naked homeless people no longer scare you.

No matter what happens to or around you, New York City will teach you to take everything in stride.

Nothing is a big deal. So even if something is a big deal, you are well aware that you must act as if it isn't. In other words, the best reaction is no reaction. Unless of course, you'd like a front row seat to the one-homeless-man show entitled *Who Can I Smear Some Crap On?*

Think about it. Why scream or flinch at the sight of a bare-assed guy's junk as he does squat-thrusts up and down the aisle of your subway car, allowing his genitalia to touch the floor, when you can just get off at the next stop?

Problem solved.

64. Seriously, though, nothing surprises you.

People fully dressed as wizards walking casually among the crowd. A guy on a unicycle pushing a single speaker past an acrobatics team that tells inappropriate racial jokes between flips and a pervasive marijuana scent in the air at all times.

So what?

Some guy standing alongside the FDR, holding a plastic baby and empty bottle of Thunderbird, sporting an old Burger King paper crown, would be worth talking about—except that before you have an opportunity to mention it to anyone, you'll see so much more.

It really does take the unimaginable to imagine shaking your imagination. Imagine that.

65. *You continuously say how much you hate people and you're not kidding.*

Your friend folder is full and the newly introduced have to run the gauntlet for you to even consider allowing them into your inner circle. Your exclusivity policy used to be a running joke. Now, it's no laughing matter.

Why open yourself up to the risk?

You've seen enough, learned enough, and learned the hard way enough to know you're correct to assume the worst about people on sight. Okay, not the worst—just that you probably won't like them enough to hang out again.

Besides, it's not as if they know how you feel or anything. And if they did, they probably wouldn't even care.

That thought alone makes you a little more skeptical of them, because clearly they have no idea what they're missing.

66. *You despise tourists.*

You have no patience for the crowds or what they're wearing. You point to your headphones if one of those stop-and-stare, Red Lobster–eaters dares to ask you for directions. And if one more of them stops short on the middle of the sidewalk to look up and point at the Empire State Building, you may just have to tell them where they really need to go.

You simply don't have the time for people who don't know what they're doing or where they're going. The problem is that there are more of them than you. However, you know the rules of walking, shopping, ordering, and general New York City decorum.

They don't even know the rules exist. Stupid tourists.

67. Everyone has started to look a little odd.

You're always surrounded by people and bumping into people, while trying to act as though you don't notice people at all.

But lately, you've started noticing every flaw and quirk and atypical curve. You take note of the beauty marks, freckles, and big white teeth, as well as the perfect necklines. Differences are what make individuals individual.

Then there's the other, more critical side of your observational skills.

Your mean streak has gotten significantly broader. You're also noticing hairy shoulders, huge foreheads, nervous tics, and big noses. (You get the picture.) Internally, you dismantle and deconstruct them all with extreme prejudice to entertain yourself during your commute to and from work.

New York has taught you unique can be beautiful. But this city has also taught you that part of beauty is knowing what to cover up and what to highlight. Anyone who doesn't know that deserves to be teased. Or at least, that's what you've been telling yourself.

68. You're so judgmental you've begun to look down on yourself.

Part of being a New York City–styled know-it-all, seen-it-all type is knowing how to *do* it better as well.

Call it the evolution of a smartass, but while mistakes, general miscues, and social faux pas happen, you know if everybody did what you said in the first place, they wouldn't happen nearly as often.

Forget suffering fools lightly. You don't suffer them at all.

Missteps are greeted with much contempt. Usually silently, since a look of disbelief and disdain will do just fine. But you, too, stumble on occasion. When you do, you beat yourself up for something that really doesn't warrant it, wondering how you went wrong and laboring over the cost of the perceived transgression. All this and it's only Monday morning.

69. The smart people aren't really people-people.

There are countless well-read, informed, and brilliant people in New York City. But often times, they're not the cool I-just-happen-to-know type. They're of the I-know-and-how-could-you-not? variety.

You find that arrogance worthy of an open-handed Tae Kwon Do chop to the throat. But in the time it takes to rewind and replay the incident in your mind, to identify just how and when they took an intellectual swipe at you, they've gotten away.

You're not perturbed because they know something you may not. It's just that they leave you to wonder: why do they have to be so damned condescending?

NOTE: If this particular entry doesn't ring true or seem familiar to you, there is a high likelihood that you are one of the smart, non-people-people who inspired this entry.

70. That person over there won't stop staring at you.

Do they want to fight you? Or do they want to screw you?

Whether male or female, that's what it comes down to, because you just never know. There's always someone looking, lurking, and noticing you just enough for you to notice them.

Some days, it's annoying; on others, it's a little more sinister. Yet with so many people around, and so many places to be and times to be there, how is it that this potential weirdo is so close, so often? Why isn't this person as enamored with anyone else?

Not that you mind attention; you just don't know what kind of attention you're getting. Is it Mr. or Mrs. Right pondering a charming introduction, or a documentary-bound serial killer studying your every move? You'll find out soon enough.

71. *You honk the moment before the light turns green.*

You have to walk up the escalator. Old people are always in your way. You'll even squeeze into a train car that's well past capacity even though the conductor has informed you that "there is another train directly behind this one." The fact is, you're always in a hurry.

You're in a rush to do things and be places of which you really want no part.

But you'll consider all that a little more deeply after you get there and scope out the situation. For now, you're just praying the guy in the wheelchair waiting at the next bus stop will take the next bus, so you don't have to wait the extra seven minutes it will take for the driver to get him onboard.

72. *If you wanted to be phony, you'd live in L.A.*

Los Angeles is on the other side of the map and on the other end of the spectrum for a reason. It's La-La Land, Hollywood—you know, plastic. But New York City is supposed to be the real thing, not just a reasonable facsimile.

Yet you've discovered that the world-renowned, quickly recognized, iconic New York City way of being is becoming more performance than personality. Especially since over half of the city's residents aren't actually from New York.

You've taken note of how the avant-garde, unapologetic, truthful soul of the city is fading and being replaced by a stylish, commercial, eco-friendly surface that looks the same, but just isn't what it's pretending to be.

But New York City isn't the land of make believe. It's the land of *make it happen.*

73. *You've realized Brooklyn is just as pretentious as Manhattan.*

The rent is about the same. The babies have two mommies. The babies have two daddies. And in some cases, the babies have a sixty-year-old mommy and daddy. Interracial couples are the norm.

In fact, if you're with someone of the same race, nationality, and religion, you're looked at with a touch of confusion.

You can actually hear yourself think. It's still dangerous, industrial, and unfinished in pockets. The art is still undiscovered. The music is fresh. And everyone knows it!

There's a distinctive and non-too-subtle I-know-a-secret swagger and sway present in the way Brooklyners do it. And it would be okay if they'd admit it was the case. But

that wouldn't be very progressively hipster, upscale casual,
pretentiously unpretentious, now would it?

74. Trying to look busy is exhausting work.

You're always either on your phone or on your way to a
meeting. You're either texting or chatting. You're either out
or getting ready to go out. You're either on a date or on the
prowl for your next one. You're either reflecting on last week
or planning for next week. Heading to the train or reading on
it. You're always doing something, needed for something, and
making something happen.

But in New York, the only thing more important than
being in the act of doing something is simply looking as
though you are. And when you stop to think about it, it's kind
of nuts… but luckily for you, you don't usually have time to
stop to think about it because you're too busy looking busy.

75. (Unwritten) Rules, (Unwritten) Rules, (Unwritten) Rules.

Anything does not go. Anything may have gone in the
past, but not now.

The city does sleep. Approximately from 6:00 a.m. to
8:15 a.m. on Sunday mornings.

Talent can only get you so far.

All that glitters is gold. But gold is heavy, and people
kill each other to get it.

Just putting yourself out there is not enough.

It's not that easy to get around.

76. People don't dance; at least, not like they used to.

Dancing is freedom. Freedom is dancing. (Don't act as if you haven't seen *Footloose*.) Maybe it's because there are no judgments. Or maybe it's because fun and charmingly innocent sexuality reign supreme.

The cabaret laws didn't do in dancing. The too-cool-for-school crowd did. Things have become more imitation than revolution and more retro than innovation.

The inconsistency and sparseness of crowded, bustling dance floors, with people actually dancing on them, is one place it shows up quite clearly.

Maybe no one is letting loose because it's hard to let go when you're concerned with how it looks rather than how it feels. But that's nothing a good dance can't fix.

77. You're thinking about the future. Not just your future, but "the" future.

There was a time when every question you asked was about *me, myself,* and *I.* But now, your questions are about *we, us,* and *our.* You've become increasingly more conscious of things that exist beyond what you want and where you're going.

You're interested in discovering and sharing the type of intellectual understanding and spiritual growth capable of elevating the lives of those you love and those you've never even met.

And while that's a lovely sentiment, New York City survival is based on self. Whatever your motivation, and regardless of how you go about it, this is an *I* town. If you're in the game and playing for keeps, *I* is all you have and the only thing you are responsible for. When *I* falls down your list of priorities and personal gain no longer means everything, you may find you need more room to grow.

And in New York City, real estate isn't easy to come by.

78. *Your worth means more than your wealth.*

With all the things you've seen and done, New York City has refined your point of view, sharpened your senses, and given you a perspective about life and living. That's a good thing.   But as you worked and played and got really good at doing both, you stopped once or twice to take in the view. Or maybe you were such a good student you learned on the fly.

Either way, your value system has become more valuable to you. Things like *stuff, money,* and *status* mean less than esteem, righteousness, and the ability to look at yourself in the mirror without shame, disgust, or horror.

Of course, you could clean up your act in New York City. But it is considerably easier to backslide when you're always climbing uphill.

79. *You have kids now.*

No non–New York born, New York parent wants to send their child to school through a hole in the ground. The symbolism is far too glaring to be ignored. There's no age of innocence for the youth; no space to grow up, spread out, and live and learn as a kid.

For the average New Yorker of average New York City means, backyards and extra rooms are nonexistent. Parks are field trips, and grass is hard to find. Kids don't really get to be kids in New York, and since you weren't born and raised here, it just doesn't seem natural. It doesn't seem good enough for them.

Not to mention that nursery and private schools cost as much, if not more, than college will, but at least you have eighteen years to save for that. And when the thought of it all hits you like a bag full of husky pencils and construction paper, all you want is some juice, a cookie, and a nice long nap.

80. *You're not screwed up enough to be here anymore.*

At first glance, everyone comes to New York City for all the right reasons. However, secretly, something slightly less beautiful often inspires the pilgrimage.

New York City is an escape from a town that's too small or too small minded. It's an escape from a family that could be absent, unsupportive, or just a little uninspired. It's an escape from an existence that isn't as meaningful as your gut tells you it should be or was meant to be.

In short, you're all screwed up, in one way or another, and so you came to a place where being screwed up is a prerequisite.

That sense of destiny, ego, stubbornness, and blind ambition drives you. It helps you find a piece of the peace you've always been looking for. But your once razor-sharp edge has gone dull, as wounds healed and misdeeds were understood and forgiven, if not forgotten.

Now, you find yourself wondering aloud, "Why is everybody so mad?" You accept the simple truth that you used to be a card-carrying member of the always-frustrated, always-searching, always-trying-to-prove-a-point New York crowd.

You're just not one of them anymore.

81. Less has become more.

You want less criticism, less noise, less distraction, less competition, less stress, less stuff, less attention, less mystery and less doubt.

Less? Less. Less!

You don't want to stop and smell the roses. You want to plant, nurture, and prune them. You even want to name the roses and spend every waking moment amongst them. But that's not an option here. New York City is frenetic, and even when you rationalize and prioritize it as best you know how, you're still traveling at a pace that would disorient most.

Basically, rose gardens require more time than you have to give. So how much more time are you thinking you might need?

82. Homesickness.

For many reasons, some selfish and some soulful, it's time to go home. You can hear the call and you've stopped trying to block it out. It's comfortable, it's familiar, and it's when and where the dream started, and now you want to go back.

New York is a dangerous, sexy lover, out on the town, dancing the night away, and drinking you under the table. Home makes sure your kids don't eat dessert for breakfast, puts money away for a rainy day, and volunteers at the local shelter.

If you no longer require an intense fire with your desire, a change back to what you once knew might be in order. After all, by now you've probably gotten what you came for, whether you recognize it or not.

83. "The Secret", "The Dream Giver", and "A New Earth" have done nothing for you.

You're not quite sure of your special purpose. Boo-frigginhoo! Get out of *Barnes and Noble* and get back into the real world.

The very process of attempting to find yourself and your so-called purpose in New York City is the secret, living the dream, and discovering a new earth.

Simply by being here, you're standing on the **X** that marks the spot. New York City isn't about choosing correctly. It's about choosing something and going from there. Because like no place else, *Guess who I met today? Can you believe that happened?*, and *What are the odds?* all call New York City home.

However, you can't be consumed by *if, how,* and *when* and love New York at the same time. You merely have to keep the faith, assuming you can find a little.

84. You're all grown up.

Birthdays have come and gone. Leases have been signed and broken. Relationships have lived fast and died hard. Jobs have been taken and given back. Your hair is thinning, graying, or finding new places to sprout.

You've become fond of saying "if I knew then what I know now," and there's nothing more thrilling than knowing your rent is paid in advance. You've more than come full circle. You've begun a new one.

New York City has been pretty good to you and was pretty good for you. So why not quit while you're ahead? Cash out. Leave them wanting more. You could. But that wouldn't be very New York of you, and you know it.

85. You have an exit strategy.

Any meaningful and necessary military exercise should include a well-conceived endpoint and a method of withdrawal. Being the good general you are, you have a plan. The time has come for you to put it into action.

Whether your New York story is one of *veni, vidi, vici* or the little engine that never quite did, the clock is dangerously close to midnight on your Cinderella story. Maybe it's time to pull up stakes and get the hell out of Dodge. Because to be in this city, it has to be in you, and an exit plan means it's not.

Yes, it's smart. Yes, it's practical. But by definition alone, it's not New York.

86. A complete lack of inspiration.

Walking the streets of New York City used to be all the inspiration you required. A breakthrough of some kind was always just around the corner. Maybe it was an answer or just a new way of asking questions.

Your enthusiasm and energy fueled your hope and faith.

Every sunset on the Brooklyn Bridge, every Whitney exhibition, every new person, every new assignment, and every conversation sparked a potentially humongous idea.

Some you saw to fruition and some weren't properly incubated, but the next big thing never felt far away.

You just knew that when—not if—it happened, it would surely be the flawless culmination of all that came before it.

Now, it seems the *next* has become the *not*, and the *be-all-to-end-all* has simply ended. So is that silence surrounding you the sound of the fat lady preparing to sing, or is it just a brief intermission in the show?

87. You're plain and you're fine with it.

It should come as no surprise that a city known as the melting pot is all about flavor.

So, do you appreciate the ethnic, religious, social (and every other conceivable type of) diversity it has to offer? Are you actively contributing to it? If you're not, you will be deemed bland and boring, and there's no excuse for that. There's no tolerance for it either.

So take a continuing education class. Learn a foreign language. Visit the nearest hobby shop. Join a social club, better yet, start one of your own. Perform in the streets. Sing for your supper.

Do something to make yourself worthy of your spot in this city. It's never too late, if you're willing. Otherwise this city will pass you by and pass you up, assuming it hasn't already.

88. No love.

New York City is the spiritual and geographic nexus of personal freedom, creative expression, and boundless opportunity. Its coordinates are the exact spot on the globe where anything might occur and everything is completely possible. Yet you're living an existence to the contrary.

You can't find anything about this city or anyone in it to fall completely in love with, or enough varying items to illicit crush after adult crush. It is quite possible your time

has come. But what it's come to and where it's going are
still up for debate.

89. *You watch reruns.*

There's too much going on here to watch television.
There's certainly too much going on here to watch the
same thing more than once.

There's some appointment viewing deserving of
water-cooler and industry-party talk. There are the guilty
pleasures we occasionally indulge in, which we mention
in carefully monitored tones. That you'd rather watch
and re-watch them than explore the greatest city on the
face of the planet is an opportunity lost, thirty to sixty
minutes at a time.

90. *It's about damn time.*

The grass is always greener on the other side, but New
York City is primarily asphalt.

So everything looks better by comparison. You've
decided you may need another way of doing, being, seeing,
and living. New York City isn't some evil force pushing,
shredding, and grinding you at every turn, even though it
can feel that way from time to time.

It's a thorn in the side, a burr under the saddle, and a
piece of gravel in your shoe.

Strangely enough, you are fully aware that New York
City is also the magical elixir capable of making all the

pain disappear. But you've grown weary of the constant pushing and pulling and no longer find any sadomasochistic pleasure in the highs and lows.

Basically, the inspiration has fallen prey to the perspiration. And you probably never even saw it coming.

91. You pass time by counting pay periods.

The fifteenth and the thirty-first give you a charge. They are your monetary keys to the city. You need cash to grease the wheels of the machine. Nothing compares to getting paid, and that goes double in New York City.

Free can be fun. But you get what you pay for.

Still, none of that is why you do it. You just want and need to have something to look forward to. It's just a little more hopeful than the X's on a jail cell calendar, but the idea is essentially the same.

If *trapped* or *boxed in* describe your New York City state of mind, it's time for you to fly the coop. Two weeks at a time is no way to measure life, especially in a city that's as alive as this one. Either find a new way to pass time or find a new pastime.

92. New York has become too New York, even for New York.

You've come to know this city. Not just where stuff is, but how things go. In your understated, nuanced wisdom, you recognize the difference between true grit and bullshit.

At this point, you could probably teach a masterclass on poser spotting, because you know an advertising executive disguised as a scruffy-faced, weathered, leather-jacket-wearing Harley rider when you see one. You know a three-legged dog is more a fashion accessory than a rescue mission. You recognize how people are acting like they live in New York instead of actually *living* like they live in New York. To most it goes unnoticed, but you're incapable of turning a blind eye. You're not enjoying it as much as you once did, because you see how New York City has become more of a knockoff than the real thing, in all the ways that really mean something to you. And you're having a hard time seeing the humor in that.

93. Outside dining.

Regardless of season, temperature, and, to some degree, the food, you'll eat outside just because you see a table. A table on the sidewalk and an opportunity to snatch one up is like recess, naptime, and a stirring game of red-light-green-light all wrapped up into one neat aluminum-foil swan.

It's oh-so-New York, oh-so-fabulous, and oh-so-ridiculous.

If you're actually taking time to think about what you're doing and what it all means, rather than making reservations, asking about the specials, reviewing wine lists, and indulging in every morsel of the moment, it may be time to ask for the check.

94. Re-entry.

New York City is fantastic. Yet, of late, you've begun to say you *have to* and *need to* vacation more than you say you'd simply *like to*. You love being here, but you love saying *I'm out of here* more and more every day.

Leaving for a day, a week, or a month provides an opportunity to decompress. It's a rare chance to let your guard down and breathe freely. So you do. But just as you really start to get into it, the pilot, conductor, driver, or captain announces, "Welcome back to New York!" And though you try your damnedest to brace yourself and hold onto everything you hold dear throughout the spiritual turbulence, it's jarring and it burns.

It is re-entry.

The only way to avoid it is to leave and never come back. For a true New Yorker, that's just not an option. So ask yourself, are you still a true New Yorker?

95. You're making more money than you ever thought you would and it's still not enough.

It's not greed or selfishness. It's both. Plus the reality of how expensive New York City truly is.

But you survived as an entry-level associate with three roommates and no cable connection. You did just fine even though your best meals were scavenged from conference rooms after office meetings. But now, after a handful of raises and promotions and just general understanding of how to do New York City, you should be better about your money. You did well with none; surely you can do well with considerably more.

Anywhere else, you could call it human nature. The more you get, the more you want. But here, it should be referred to as *superhuman nature,* because there's considerably more to be had. Before you even get it, you have a plan for it.

No matter how far ahead you get, you're always a little behind. Maybe that's why gambling addicts refer to it as *chasing it.*

96. Smoking is making a comeback.

Not too long ago, smokers were looked down upon, judged, and banished to scurry about outside by law to indulge in their filthy habit—and rightly so.

Their smoke got into your hair, behind your eyes, and under your skin. They became social pariahs, and smoking became a relationship deal breaker to just about everyone who didn't light up.

But now, in old New York City fashion, the banned, the anti-establishment, and the generally unacceptable are cool again. Bars, speakeasies, underground clubs, and open air everywhere are being seductively corrupted by puff bandits and the nicotine-stained avengers of retro chic.

Suddenly, people are more tolerant and less offended, and the cloud continues to engulf the rest of the city. You just want to tell them to put it out. But the thing is, you know cool rules. So you breathe it in, reluctantly deciding to get your secondhand on.

97. You've gone from fringe to mainstream.

You've been underground and ahead of the curve from day one. What you loved, most people didn't know existed. You used to be so cool that people most people thought were cool looked to you to find out how to maintain their coolness. Then one day, you woke up and the world had caught up.

MTV, CNN, and even network television were on to you. Now grandmothers and Canadians nod at you knowingly as if you are part of the same secret handshaking tribe.

The worst part is you don't have any new tricks up your sleeve. You're not quite sure how it happened, but it has; your cool has become everyone's cool, and you know better than most that's not cool.

98. You have something solid elsewhere.

The ease and the conflict that exist in this muse of a city stem from knowing that nothing is definite and thus all things are possible.

In New York City, *impossible* on its most vicious, backbreaking day is at most a likelihood and never a certainty. However, the same exists for success and happiness. You just never know anything.

The prospect of security, stability, and at least a semblance of control has become more alluring. Much like how an average-looking person with good humor and a great job becomes more attractive to you than a sexy, mysterious stranger after you turn thirty-five.

New York life has taught you quite a bit. You've endured quite a few self-inflicted wounds. But you're not willing to keep hoping things will just work out anymore, because you know better.

99. You're just not loud enough.

The city is loud. The people are loud. So you need to be louder. In fact, be the loudest.

Literally and figuratively, being loud in one way or another is the only way you will ever be seen or heard. Being the loudest doesn't mean you're the best, and it certainly doesn't mean you're right. But it does give you the opportunity to get closer to the prize, because all eyes are on you and everyone is waiting to see what you'll do next.

There are too many distractions and too much surround sound to trifle with the understated. Because what chance do you really have to be successful if no one knows how much you have to offer?

100. *There's no one to blame.*

New York City is wondrous. It's not a *wonderland*.

There's no fairy dust to lift you from where you are and delicately place you on the A-list of the lifestyle of your choosing. Only elbow grease, fortuitous timing, sweat, and a little bit of luck can do that.

You can find all the materials and accessories you'll need to customize and renovate your dream right here.

As cliché as it may be, New York City is what you make of it, as much as what it makes of you. Coming here (and leaving here, for that matter) are all about the choices you make. Or, maybe more importantly, the choices you find yourself unwilling to make.

101. *You bought this book.*

Whether you're looking for a good laugh, a good thought, or a good excuse, you're looking for something.

You keep telling yourself it's in New York, but maybe it's not. If honest self-evaluation reveals a story of effort, energy, hustle, and hope, then maybe your thing isn't a part of this thing. Perhaps it never was.

Regardless, New York City has refined your talents, as well as sharpened your teeth and your tongue. Maybe that's all it was ever meant to do. Or maybe you're just getting started, and it's time to take a stance and make a stand, because just as each of the entries in this book are reasons to leave New York City, they're also reasons to stay.

But—and New York City is all about the *but*— that's for you to decide.

Hopefully, in reading this book about leaving New York City, you've rediscovered the reasons you originally came. Maybe you've even been reminded of all you can do and become by being here. Or not just by being here, but by living here, loving here, learning here, getting up, and standing out every single day.

So if you're here and you don't like what New York is doing to you or for you, leave. No harm, no foul. You've become a stronger, better person for the experience. If you're here and you have a few more ideas on how to get what you want without losing who you are, stick around and test your hypotheses. The worst thing that can happen is that you find out you're wrong. But if you're right, the possibilities truly are limitless.

If you've never been and you never come, that's fine, too. Obviously, it's not for everyone. Fear has nothing to do with it. Maybe you weren't interested before and this did nothing to whet your appetite. If you've never been and now you know it's what you want for your life, come and get it!

New York is waiting.

But it's not waiting to shake your hand and pat you on the back. It's waiting to kick your ass and run you over. And if—and only if—you get up time after time after time and brush yourself off, over and over and over again, then maybe you'll understand. Then again, maybe you won't.

Ah, New York.

CPSIA information can be obtained at www.ICGtesting.com
Printed in the USA
LVOW12s1130191013

357682LV00001B/301/P